The Scarecrow
Who Wanted a Hug

Translated by Polly Lawson
First published in Italian as *Lo spaventapasseri è innamorato!*
© 2002 Edizione Arka, Milan
English version © 2002 by Floris Books, 15 Harrison Gardens, Edinburgh
British Library CIP Data available
ISBN 0-86315-376-3
Printed in Italy

The Scarecrow
Who Wanted a Hug

Guido Visconti
Illustrated by Giovanna Osellame

Floris Books

Barnaby was a happy scarecrow.
He had many friends, especially
the birds that he was supposed
to scare away! In exchange for letting
them peck at the wheat, the birds
helped Barnaby by carrying tender
messages to Gwendoline, at the top
of the hill.

Barnaby loved Gwendoline very
much and wanted to give her a hug,
but he could only wave at her from
a distance.

With the onset of autumn Barnaby became sad. Many of his friends went away.

The soft breeze turned into the North Wind, and Barnaby worried that he would lose his hat, and Gwendoline would see that he had no hair.

But when the North Wind went away then the fog came, and Barnaby could not see Gwendoline at all.

However, Barnaby did not have much
time to admire Gwendoline in the autumn,
for he had to look out for hunters for his
remaining friends.

"Enemy coming!" he shouted when
he saw a hunter approaching with a rifle.

Then the foxes, hares, pheasants,
ducks and quails quickly disappeared
into the woods, or hid among the reeds.

Sometimes one was not quick enough ...
"Bang!" went the gun.
"Ouch!" cried the quail as she fell.

The hunter came looking for the quail but she had disappeared.

"I'm sure I hit her," he grumbled.

The more he searched the angrier, redder and hotter he became.

He took off his scarf and placed it on Barnaby's shoulder.

"Make sure that the wind doesn't blow it away," he said, then walked off still looking for the quail.

The scarf was lovely and warm.

"He's gone. You can come out now." Barnaby said to the quail, who was hiding in his pocket. "Are you hurt?"

"Not much," answered the quail. "But what can I do to thank you?"

"Could you take this scarf to Gwendoline for me? She looks a little cold up on the hill."

Quickly the quail flew to Gwendoline and gave her the scarf.

"This is with love from Barnaby," she said. "I'm sure he will marry you one of these days!"

"That would be wonderful," sighed Gwendoline, and waved to Barnaby.

But Barnaby did not see her ...

The hunter was coming back to collect his scarf. But his scarf had gone.

"You were supposed to look after it," he shouted at Barnaby. "Now I'm cold!"

He grabbed the scarecrow's hat.

"Oh, no ... I'll die of shame!" cried Barnaby, as the hunter started pulling at his jacket.

"Oh, he'll freeze to death," cried Barnaby's friends from their hiding places.

"Now it's our turn to save Barnaby," they shouted.

And the foxes, ducks, pheasants, crows, hares and quails all threw themselves at the hunter, and tripped him up.

The hunter tried to protect himself. He pulled Barnaby out of the ground and held him in front like a stick.

"This is too much," the animals snapped, and crept closer to the hunter.

The hunter tried to escape, and ran up the hill dragging Barnaby behind him.

"Help, help. Enemies at my heels!" the hunter shouted.

Barnaby's friends chased the hunter until they were almost out of breath.

"Just a bit further," shouted Barnaby. "We are nearly there!"

"You can stop here!" he cried, when they reached the top of the hill.

"Yes, please stop," agreed the hunter. "You can have your hat back, but please tell the others to leave me alone! Oh ... here's my scarf!"

And the hunter grabbed his scarf from Gwendoline's shoulders and walked off without a word of thanks.

Barnaby didn't know how to repay his friends.

"Thank you. Thank you," he stuttered.

He was in a terrible state. His clothes were all ruffled but he didn't mind. He was so happy to be close to Gwendoline. He wanted to give her a big hug, but he didn't know how.

"Let me help you," said the North Wind, and he blew Barnaby's sleeve gently over Gwendoline's shoulder.

"Now they are truly married!" he gusted to the world.

And the scarecrows lived together happily on the top of the hill, beneath the beautiful full moon.